Kreepo

JON STEFFENS

ANUCI PRESS

This is a work of fiction. Names, characters, places, and incidents either are the product of the author's imagination or are used fictitiously. Any resemblance to actual persons, living or dead, events, or locales is entirely coincidental.

Tanuci69@gmail.com

First paperback edition 2025

Anuci Press edition 2025

www.anuci-press.com

Cover Design by Ira Rat

ISBN 979-8-9919612-5-7 (paperback)

ISBN 979-8-9919612-6-4(eBook)

"Steffens writes with an untethered bluntness that is both horrifying and shocking." – Matt Micheli, author of *Two Minutes with the Devil*

"Jon Steffens brings a new voice to extreme horror that's honest and direct." – Ira Rat, author of *Hairs*

"Jon Steffens' scintillating writing style will not only channel malevolence to your mind, but convey terror to your soul!" – Proscriptor (Absu)

1

It was a cool October morning as the sun rose over a field on the outskirts of Terrell, Texas, bathing the sky in an autumnal pumpkin orange. Carnival workers, having arrived the previous night in a group of trucks, trailers, and RVs, busied themselves setting up the midway and an assortment of rides as the deep violet of night receded to the west. Crows cawed, hopping around the cookfires as a few of the women prepared a breakfast of eggs, sausage, and biscuits.

A few hundred yards north, a freight train traveling on the Texas & Pacific railroad slowed to a stop. The brakes hissed and startled a massive buzzard perched atop a nearby railroad crossing sign. The carrion bird stretched its gray wings and took flight. Roughly fifteen cars back from the locomotive, a rusted metal door slid open. Out climbed a tall, hulking man on wobbly legs. His single pack slung over his broad shoulders; the man staggered toward the carnival.

His clothes were ragged. Though the vagrant was a big, brutish man, his wrinkled blue workpants, a size too large, were only held up by a pair of dirty brown suspenders. The only other garment on his torso was a white tank top stained with enough grime it appeared gray.

By the time the vagrant was within sight of the carnies, all had paused their work and taken notice of the man. The children in the troupe, who had been playing with an excited dog moments before, hid behind their parents as the man approached. The unkempt hobo came to a stop a few feet from Cinderella Hand, an eighteen-year-old girl tending one of the fires. The dog, a trusty lurcher named Jook, was immediately at her side, growling cautiously at the stranger.

A hard-looking man slipped silently between the girl and the vagrant. The man wore a tweed flat cap and blue overalls with a white shirt beneath. Three gold rings adorned his fingers. The disheveled brute was surprised at the stealth of the man. He thought of himself as having a keen sense of his surroundings, and realized the man was only seen when he wanted to be. The hobo made a mental note.

"What can I help you with, friend," the hard man said without a smile.

"Looking for work. Name's Carl," uttered the vagrant through yellowed teeth.

"Patrick," said the man. He was Patrick Hand, patriarch of the family of Gypsy Travellers who operated many of the carnival's midway games. A man formidable in appearance, Patrick was a bareknuckle boxer in his youth. His family was all-important to him. Cinderella was his daughter, the eldest of three children. Cinderella, along with his wife Mary, son Hercules, and young daughter Serafina travelled and worked the carnival circuit with him. Patrick turned to his son, a strapping sixteen-year-old standing about ten feet behind him and said something in a language only the Gypsies could understand. Moments later a middle-aged man was among the gathered throng. He was round in the middle with dark, slicked-back hair.

"Name's Tom Edwards," he said, walking up to the drifter. "This resplendent assemblage here before you is Edwards Fun Fair. Been in my family for fifty years. I hear you're looking for work."

"I am. I like clowning, but I can help run rides, take tickets, whatever's needed. Call me Carl." The drifter smiled at the fair's owner. Between his rotting teeth, black hair pasted to the sides of his head, bald pate, and the remnants of blue and white greasepaint etched into the lines of his rough face, it would have been a ghastly sight to anyone who wasn't seasoned in this line of work.

Tom looked Carl over. "I can see you prefer clown work. Tell you what. I've got a dark ride, but no one to run it. You can do your clowning outside the ride, talking the rubes into taking a ride into Hell's Manor. You'll get 20% of what you bring in. Considering you're not green, it ain't a bad gig. The better you talk, the more you'll make. We'll call you Kreepo the Clown. What do you say?"

"Sounds fair enough. I'd like to start today." Kreepo stuck out his hand. Tom took it in a firm grip, and they shook on it. The new clown asked for a meal and place to freshen up. Everyone went back to work. Tom turned and walked back toward his trailer. Patrick met him at his door.

"Tom, I don't trust this new clown as far as I could throw him, which ain't too far looking at the size of the bastard," said Patrick.

"You Gypsies don't trust anyone. This isn't the old days. He looks rough as three-dollar pussy but give him a chance. If he can't do the work, we'll leave him here at the end of the week." Tom looked sure of himself.

"Your Gypsy granny wouldn't have trusted him either," Patrick sighed as Tom disappeared into his caravan. "Damned gorgers have no sense."

After finishing his warm meal, Kreepo was shown to his station. Hell's Manor, an old dark ride made up like a haunted house, was already set up. The hard work was already done. The clown laid a blanket down on the cold steel floor in back of the ride, behind a wall with a huge laughing skull painted on it. He figured it wasn't any worse than the train car. Sitting in the dark, Kreepo thought of nothing but violence, pain, and misery.

A highlight reel of human atrocity played on a constant loop in his mind. He was happy for moments like this, when he could concentrate on the joy suffering brought him. The clown reached into his rucksack and pulled out the severed head of a hobo who rode the rails with him the previous few days. Sitting back and closing his eyes, he pulled out his flaccid cock and began sliding it back and forth across the head's cold, stiff lips. He had a few hours until showtime.

2

After a hot shower in the bunkhouse washed away all the grime from his four-day ride, Carl dressed in the black slacks and white dress shirt given to him by Tom. Odd costume for a clown, but those were the only clothes anyone had lying around that would fit the drifter's large frame. Carl slicked back his stringy black hair, applied the white, blue, and black makeup in an unsettling whiteface motif, popped a tattered black top hat atop his head, and Kreepo was born.

The midway was bustling by nightfall. The queue for each attraction spilled into the walkway. All the games were two or three patrons deep, while the balloon dart booth run by Patrick's son Hercules proved the most popular. Kids loved the loud pop of the colorful balloons almost as much as they enjoyed destroying them with sharp projectiles. Their prizes –an array of trinkets ranging from plastic vampire fangs to rubber snakes and huge, fluorescent-colored plush monsters— didn't hurt either. Shadows bathed the space between the ring toss and rope ladder booths in inky darkness. It was from that murky gloom that Patrick watched the drifter work.

"Alright, ladies and gentlemen, boys and girls! Come on in, come on over, come up nice and close! It's the world-famous Hell's Manor, a ghastly abode the likes of which few have entered and survived! Ghoulish ghosts, malevolent monsters, all manner of curious creeps and carnivorous creatures the likes of which you've never seen before! They're all here, they're all hungry, and they're all waiting for you inside! Right this way to Hell's Manor!" Moving quickly back and forth behind the dark ride's guard rail, Kreepo proved himself more than an imposing frame and grotesque face. The spookhouse clown was a damn fine talker. A crowd gathered during his presentation, all waving tickets in his grease-painted face. Kreepo assisted a round of excited patrons into the seats of the ghost train. He turned and peered into the black abyss between booths only to find the gruff Gypsy no longer there.

The next three nights went on much the same. Kreepo was a hit. So much so, that Hell's Manor quickly became the number one attraction at the carnival. Some of the dark ride's popularity could be chalked up to the fact it was October, but the charismatic clown with the menacing appearance played a large part in the packed queue lines. Between the money the attraction was bringing in and the charisma Kreepo projected –both during work hours and afterward around the cookfires— the clown was swiftly accepted among the carnival folk. Everyone working the fair enjoyed his wild tales and lewd jokes. Everyone but Patrick.

On the last night before the show packed up for the next town, Patrick unhitched his old truck, climbed in the cab and took it into town to visit a cousin, grab a few road supplies and some sweets for Mary and the kids. He'd asked his beloved wife to ensure the children didn't leave the caravan. Normally he wouldn't be so cautious, but Patrick couldn't shake the dark feeling he had about that damned drifter. As he drove through the streets on the old side of town, he noticed tiny, run-down hovels next door to beautiful, sprawling Victorian-style homes. He wondered what the neighbors had in common or if they ever spoke to each other.

It was after midnight and all in the Hand family caravan were fast asleep. All but Cinderella. She was planning to sneak out to meet a boy, James Willis. His family ran the Ferris wheel and bumper cars. James was the first young man Cinderella had feelings for that her parents didn't entirely disapprove of, though they'd certainly be unhappy with her sneaking around at night with him. Still, she hoped her father warmed up to him a bit more. James was kindhearted, hard-working, and honest, but Patrick didn't place much trust in anyone outside of those he counted among his family.

The raven-haired girl silently crept toward the door, her steps light as to not wake her family. Cinderella stepped into the cool night, the family dog Jook wagging his tail as soon as he saw her. As she turned to walk into the darkness toward where the Willis' were camped, Jook whined. "Come on, boy," she whispered, rubbing the lightly colored fur between his dark ears. Moving as silent as the trees, the two stepped into the darkness.

A group of five carny men sat in a circle around a dying fire, Kreepo the drifter clown among them. Each took turns telling dirty jokes and regaling one another with tales of past exploits. One of the men, a gray-haired rugged old coot named Jake, talked of the time he convinced a rube to spend his entire week's pay on a ring toss game some years ago. A flash of movement in the dark caught the Kreepo's eye as he turned his head toward Hell's Manor. Whether too involved in Jake's anecdote or too drunk, none of the other men noticed.

"Well boys, I've got to piss," Kreepo said while standing up to excuse himself from the group.

"Jook, get back here!" Cinderella's words escaped her mouth in a harsh whisper. The dog took off after a rustle in the underbrush behind the dark ride. As the girl peered into the inky blackness between the trees in hope of spotting her pup, a massive, calloused hand closed over her mouth. She froze in terror as a strong arm wrapped around her waist, pulling her tight into a large body directly behind her. Jook darted from the dark. He growled, then began barking. Cinderella couldn't see Jook behind her but heard her dog's protest cut short as the bark turned into a sharp yipping, followed by a stomp and loud crunch. Tears welled in her eyes as she cried against the large fingers over her mouth.

The hand wrenched her head back. Cinderella, now looking toward the sky, saw only the ghastly white makeup of the drifter clown. He lowered his face until his lips nearly touched her nose.

"Utter one goddamn sound, and I'll snap your fucking neck, bitch."

3

Cinderella was in hell. Kreepo had carried the girl into the back of the dark ride and roughly shoved her against the wall. A solitary black light mounted above a fluorescent green foam skull bathed the space in an ugly purple glow. The scents of latex and rot mixed to assault her sense of smell. Though strands of her dark hair hung in front of her face, it wasn't enough to obscure the ghastly sight of the drifter clown's grinning visage.

"I'm going to move my hand. If you scream or try to fight, it will be the last bad decision you ever make," the clown grumbled through a deranged smile. "Do you understand?"

Cinderella tried to nod slowly as she steadied her breathing.

"Good cunt." Kreepo relaxed his grip and moved his hand from her mouth. "So, what's your defect, girl? Aren't you Gypsy cows all married off by thirteen? You're an old whore by pikey standards."

"My father says he won't let me wed anyone but a proper man, Traveller or otherwise." Cinderella stood straight, trying to appear proud and unafraid, but her uncontrollable shivering gave her away. "And none are around."

The clown slapped the girl across the face hard enough to daze her. "Bitch, I'm the best man you'll ever have." With a steel grip he grabbed her chin, yanking open her mouth. Kreepo shoved three dirty fingers down her throat, stretching her lips. Tears ran down her cheeks as she gagged and vomited. The clown removed his fingers and wiped his hand in her hair as Cinderella fell to the ground, retching. The contents of her stomach spilled from her mouth, pooling around her crying face.

Kreepo laughed. It sounded like rusty nails being dropped into an ashtray. "There you go. Let it all out for daddy."

"Why are you doing this?" Cinderella looked up at him through a choking sob.

Kneeling until his grotesque white face was close enough to hers that she could smell his rancid breath, Kreepo whispered "Girl, I'm just getting started."

Kreepo flipped the girl onto her back. Her hair soaked in vomit; she begged him to let her go home. The clown laughed at first, then grew annoyed. He again placed a large hand over her mouth as he pulled up her skirt with the other. Cinderella struggled, but it proved useless against the clown's strength. With one hand, he ripped the blue cotton panties from her body. Urine leaked from the terrified girl. It only served to further excite Kreepo.

The clown ran his fingers through the vomit on the floor until he felt they were sufficiently coated. With a quick jabbing motion, he plunged the same three fingers used to gag the girl into her vagina. Cinderella squirmed and clawed at him, screaming against his hand, but he easily held her in place. He stretched her, adding his pinky finger, then the tip of his thumb. He pressed hard, feeling her flesh give way as his knuckles finally slid inside her. Cinderella went still, her eyes blankly staring at the ceiling as he began violently pummeling her insides with his right fist. Blood mixed with her vaginal fluid as he had nearly his entire forearm inside the catatonic girl. When he was satisfied with his efforts, he pulled his hand free. More urine, blood, and mucous spilled from her ruined orifice.

Kreepo removed his left hand from her mouth and stared at the girl. Cinderella, still staring at the metal ceiling of the trailer that served as Hell's manor, began whispering something repeatedly. The clown leaned in to listen and realized she was repeating a prayer.

"That won't do at all," Kreepo frowned.

He placed four fingers into her mouth and his thumb beneath her chin. The clown lifted Cinderella's head and bashed her skull into the trailer's metal floor repeatedly until the girl stopped moving. As the clown loosened his grip, the back of her shattered skull hit the floor with a wet slap.

The way Cinderella's vacant eyes stared upward at nothing made Kreepo rock hard. He unzipped and dropped his filthy pants. The clown fucked the girl's battered, lifeless body, driving his pelvis into hers with brute force until he unloaded inside her corpse. Less than two minutes after he started, Kreepo tossed what was left of Cinderella Hand out the back door of the Hell's Manor trailer. Her body hit the dirt with a thud, coming to rest next to the remains of Jook.

Ten minutes later he was a mile down the road, heading northeast on FM 986. Kreepo had stolen the truck, with Hell's Manor towing behind. His thoughts were full of blood and cum.

4

Patrick pulled onto the carnival grounds sometime after one in the morning. He immediately noticed something was off. Too many people were awake and moving about with flashlights in hand. Patrick parked his truck near a crowd of carnies looking toward something on the ground. As he exited the vehicle, he heard an unmistakable wail.

It was Mary, her voice shuddering with intense grief. Patrick pushed his way to the center of the mass of people. When he saw it his knees buckled, and he fell to the ground. In her arms, Mary hand cradled the lifeless body of her and Patrick's beloved daughter Cinderella.

Their sweet baby girl had been utterly brutalized. Her broken head so smashed and swollen they could barely see their daughter in the cold, twisted lump of battered flesh. Still, it was Cinderella all the same, and she was gone. Patrick scooted toward Mary and embraced his wife. This brought on a fresh wave of body-wracking sobs, and they both cried over their dead daughter.

"I'm so sorry I left you alone, my baby girl." The pain was plain in Patrick's soft voice.

Eventually, a few of their fellow carny folk convinced Mary to leave Cinderella there with Patrick to see to Serafina and Hercules. Patrick sat there and wept over his lost child, rocking her remains back and forth, humming a sweet tune he sang to her when she was a baby. Tom Edwards stood there, unmoving. A tear rolled down his cheek as he watched this man –a hard as nails Gypsy boxer he'd known his entire life—cry like he hoped he would never have to.

Just before dawn, Patrick placed Cinderella gently on the ground and stood. Tom approached Patrick cautiously.

"Patrick, my friend. I'm sorry, I should have listened," Tom's voice was barely above a whisper.

"But you didn't." Patrick was looking in Tom's direction, but his dark eyes stared through the carnival owner. "And now she's gone."

Tom looked toward his own feet in shame. "You're right, and I'll go to my grave knowing it's my fault your little girl is dead. I'll also do everything in my power to ensure justice is done. I think I already know your answer, but do you want me to call the sheriff?"

"No muskers, Tom. You know we handle our own." The look Patrick gave the carnival owner was enough to end the conversation.

The next day, the hand family drove Cinderella's body to a secluded thicket of trees outside town. Relations to the Hands, Gypsy Travellers from the Smith, Wilson and Powers families showed up to the spot in the woods in droves. Rows of white pickup trucks towing caravans, and even an old style vardo –an intricately painted and decorated Gypsy wagon—were parked in a field nearby.

Patrick had dug a hole for his daughter early that morning. They laid the girl to rest in her mother's favorite dress, then an ornate wooden cross and floral arrangement was placed on the grave. After many asked for forgiveness from God for past transgressions, the mourners departed. Hercules led Serafina by the hand to their cousin's caravan, and they were driven back to the carnival grounds. Patrick and Mary stayed to mourn and pray over their daughter. A light breeze caressed them both, as if trying to comfort the couple.

The two sat in silence for hours. Eventually, Mary spoke. "You know I don't believe vengeance is a righteous act." Mary wiped the latest round of tears from her husband's face. "But you have to make this right, my love."

"Nothing will make this right, Mary." Patrick was stone faced. "Our little girl is gone. Nothing will ever be right again."

"You're right, but I know this will eat at you for the rest of your life if you don't handle it." Mary's eyes held nothing but love for Patrick. "It will ruin you if you don't do what needs to be done."

Patrick gazed at the woman he loved. His face was stoic though his heart screamed and wept. "You have my word."

5

The sun was sinking behind the live oak trees as Kreepo pissed into a creek at the edge of a stretch of forested land near Poetry, Texas. A mammoth-sized alligator snapping turtle surfaced a few feet from where he stood. After putting his dick back in his pants, the clown pulled a half empty pint of rotgut vodka from his pocket and chugged what was left. Kreepo eyed the reptile with the same contempt he felt for every living thing he encountered. He whipped the empty bottle at the beast, bouncing it off the turtle's shell with a satisfying *thunk.* The ancient thing sank into the murky water, disappearing beneath its shimmering black surface.

Back in the truck, Kreepo thought about his next move. He knew the dark ride he stole wasn't exactly inconspicuous, and the law would come calling. Police always ended up looking for him wherever he went. After mulling it over, Carl Kreepo made his plans. He'd have fun the next day or so playing in rural East Texas, then ditch the dark ride. He'd simply park it, burn it, hop the nearest train, and be long gone. On to the next place.

Kreepo thought about the house he saw about a half mile back the way he came as he rifled through the truck's cab for weapons. The clown put on two black leather gloves, pocketed two knives, and grabbed a heavy flashlight. Though it had gotten dark, Kreepo figured he wouldn't need the flashlight, but felt he should bring it anyway. It had a nice weight to it, and even if he didn't need it to see in the dark, it could be good for some blunt-force trauma.

The truck door creaked softly as Kreepo eased it shut. Light bathed the clown from behind just as the latch clicked into place followed by the familiar sound of a gun's hammer locking into place. The clown froze.

"Turn around nice and slow, friend," came a voice as rough and worn as the gravel covering the dirt road below. "I don't recognize you, your truck, or whatever rig you're pulling, and I know everyone around these parts."

Slowly, Kreepo turned. His hands raised; he still grasped the flashlight. Wearing a white tank top with a good amount of his whiteface makeup rubbed off, he looked every inch the hobo clown he was.

"What the hell is wrong with your face?" The old man held his own light steady. In his right hand was a Smith & Wesson 686, pointed right at Kreepo's gut. "That clown paint?"

"Yes sir," said Kreepo, as sheepishly as his hulking frame would allow. He could tell that even though the old man was cautious, he had no fear of Carl. A lifetime of hard work, military service, and being Texan had made the old buzzard a brave one. Slouching to seem a bit smaller, Kreepo played to the man's self-confidence perfectly. "Just got off a carnival job, on to the next town. I got lost on these back roads, and my truck broke down."

The old man squinted, still eyeing Kreepo with suspicion. After a moment's pause, he lowered the revolver slightly. "I see," he said slowly. "Well, hand me the blades you just slipped into your pocket and hop in my truck. We'll go get my tools and a light."

"Sounds fair." Kreepo's grin was friendly considering his brutish face, though his eyes were ice cold. He handed over his two beat-up knives to the old man.

The pair exited the old man's truck back at his place, gravel crunching beneath their boots in an eerie harmony. The air felt heavy and still. Kreepo followed the aged vet by a few steps as he stepped into his dark garage and flipped the light switch. A single bulb bathed the walls lined with hand tools and garden implements in a flickering yellow glow.

"Hey friend," the man said without turning around, "I didn't get your name—"

His words ended with a sickening crunch as Kreepo palmed the back of his head and smashed the old man's face into the wall at full force. The man limply hit the ground in a heap, his lips and nose smashed and split into a bloody mess. Crimson ran down the wall where his face connected.

A scream pierced the air—high-pitched and panicked. The codger's wife, a frail woman with silver hair, stood in the doorway leading inside the home to the elderly couples' kitchen, her eyes wide with terror. Kreepo smiled as he locked eyes with the woman. Shivering, she looked like a fawn on wobbly legs in the presence of a lion.

The clown tilted his head slightly. "Don't make this any harder than it has to be, lady," he sneered, his voice dripping with malice and contempt. The old woman turned and tried to run, but Kreepo was on her in two quick strides. He grabbed her by the shoulder, spun her around with ease and cracked her in the jaw with just enough force to knock her unconscious.

The woman came to, realizing she was stark naked and tied to a chair in their garage. Seated directly across from her was her husband Earl, also nude and bound. His grey hair disheveled, Earl's face now looked ten years older than the 78 years of life he'd weathered.

"Margerie, it's going to be alright, sweetheart." Earl's voice was shaky and unsure. Margerie could tell he was trying to hold back tears. In their 55 years together, she'd only seen Earl cry once, at his mother's funeral.

"No, it's not, Margerie. Nothing is ever going to be alright again," Kreepo said, stepping behind Earl. He laughed. It was an ugly sound.

Reaching over Earl's shoulder, he grabbed the old man's penis, stretching it to its full length. In a flash, Kreepo sliced off the member and tossed it in Margerie's lap. Earl grunted in pain, stifling a scream. Blood poured from the ragged gash where Earl's manhood once was. It stained his legs crimson, falling to the floor with a sound like the first drops of a heavy rain hitting concrete.

Margerie screamed uncontrollably as Kreepo moved toward her. The madman wrenched her thighs apart, Earl's severed penis slid from its perch atop her legs, hitting the seat of the chair with a faint plop.

"Don't touch her, motherfucker!" A string of drool danced on the end of his chin as Earl raged, straining against the ropes holding him hostage.

Kreepo laughed, his bloodlust building. "Margerie, that is one nice pussy, young lady," the clown said joyfully. Holding one of her legs tight, he picked up the floppy member and shoved it inside her vagina until it disappeared. "A gift, my sweet." Kreepo smiled like a hyena at Margerie's screaming, her frail voice growing ragged.

"That's it, keep singing for me." Kreepo wrapped Margerie's hair in his left fist and pulled her head back far enough she stared at the ceiling, tears running down her wrinkled cheeks. He worked steadily with Earl's favorite folding knife. Like an experienced butcher, Kreepo carved off the woman's face. Blood flowed down Margerie's neck, covering her breasts and stomach. The sound of her screams died out as haggard bursts of air emitted from her mouth.

Kreepo turned, his brutish face showing through what little of his makeup remained. Earl was facing the floor, weeping. Gripping the old man's bottom jaw, Kreepo yanked his chin upward, so their eyes met.

"Now you two can be together," Kreepo mocked as he lifted Margerie's face toward Earl's.

"I'll see you in hell, cocksucker," Earl spat at his captor.

"That's the spirit," the haggard clown chuckled as he knocked the old man's chair backward. Still tied to the chair with the air knocked from his lungs, Earl could barely struggle as Kreepo straddled his chest and plopped Margerie's face over Earl's. The old man wheezed as his tormentor sat his full weight directly on Earl's chest. Kreepo reached down near his left foot and picked up the old bow saw that fell to the garage floor during the scuffle caused by dragging Margerie into the garage. The clown placed the teeth of the rusted blade against the wrinkled skin of Earl's neck and went to work. A pained scream quickly became wet gurgles as Kreepo sawed through the old man's neck, blood gushing in bursts matching Earl's heartbeat until his head was completely removed.

Kreepo stood, holding Earls head by the hair, the old man's face still obscured by the flayed visage of his wife. "What do you old fucks think? A good night's work, I'd say," said Kreepo, his voice stained with malevolence.

Margerie, still seemingly unconscious or in shock, wheezed quietly. Kreepo dropped Earl's head to the garage floor where it landed with a wet thud. He then picked up a roofing hammer from the concrete and smashed the elderly woman in the skull four times.

Afterward, Kreepo let himself into their home and took his first hot shower in days. He then went through the couple's closet and dressed himself in Earl's finest suit. It was forest green over a white shirt. Kreepo picked out a bright red tie. While the two weren't exactly the same size, Earl was a fairly large man, so the suit fit well enough.

Rifling through Margerie's vanity drawers, Kreepo found what he needed: a black eyeliner pencil and jar of white setting powder. He sat at Margerie's mirror and created a face that was all extremes of black and white; just "clown" enough to be something almost recognizable, but off and unsettling in a way that would make passersby deeply uncomfortable. As he looked into the mirror, he didn't see Carl. No, the brutish drifter was something mundane. There was no more Carl. The thing staring back from those black pits for eyes was purely Kreepo.

"Time for one more show. It's gonna be a real doozy." The thing in the mirror smiled a rictus grin.

6

Trees lined both sides of the dirt road that led through the river bottoms, forming a canopy blocking out enough of the late-afternoon sun that the underbrush and weatherbeaten path were bathed in an otherworldly glow. Halloween had arrived.

Crystal Wells marched along the packed clay of the old road with her two boys, Caleb and Colin, in tow. Caleb, Crystal's toe-headed six-year-old, was dressed as a skeleton, while Colin, a strapping boy of eleven already familiar with the rigors of farm life, wore his school football uniform, pads and all.

"Mom, why couldn't we have taken the truck to Granny's house," Colin said, obviously annoyed.

"The brakes are shot, baby," Crystal answered her son. "Besides, Granny lives less than two miles from our front door if we take this shortcut through the bottoms, and we could all use the exercise with the amount of candy we're gonna eat!"

"Yay! Candy!" Caleb was ecstatic. "What is that music, Mommy?"

Coming from just ahead, the trio could hear Bach's "Toccata and Fugue in D minor" in ominous pipe organ over what sounded like the whir of a gas generator. Less than one hundred feet up the road, a gargantuan figure stepped from the underbrush and stopped in the middle of the path. The figure spread its arms and appeared to smile. It was a clown.

Crystal and the boys stood with their jaws agape. This wasn't your typical birthday clown, but a tall, hulking figure dressed in a fine green suit with a red tie and shiny black shoes. Adorned with a black top hat, his face was an amalgamation of stark white and inky black, giving him slitted pits for eyes and a sinister, full-lipped smile.

"Come one, come all! Boys and girls, step right up and experience the thrills and chills of the spookiest ride mortal man can handle on this All Hallow's Eve!" Kreepo gestured dramatically to Hell's Manor, fully set up just off the road to his left. Colin and Caleb shrieked with excitement and broke into a run toward the clown.

"Boys, wait!" Crystal ran after her sons. She quickly caught up, grabbing Caleb's wrist just before he reached for the clown's hand. "Sir, what is this? Why is there a carnival ride set up way out here in the middle of nowhere? The river bottoms aren't exactly in town."

"Excellent question, my dear!" Kreepo attempted a human smile. "The fair I travel with is on its way to Quinlan, but I arrived in the area before the rest of the midway workers. The bossman said I ought to set up on my own to drum up business. I figured this remote spot was perfect for a haunted house-themed attraction."

"Mommy! Can we go in the spookhouse? *Pleeeaaaassse*?" Caleb looked up at his mother with excited saucer eyes.

Crystal thought it over. "How much?" She eyed the clown with suspicion.

"Free of charge, ma'am." The clown used his most professional tone. "Just hoping you and your boys will enjoy it and come see us in the next town."

"How about it, Colin? Do you want to try the spookhouse?" Crystal looked to her older son.

"Yeah, sure." The boy was genuinely intrigued. "Let's do it!"

"Alright mister, uh, what's your name?" Crystal asked the clown.

"You can call me Kreepo, ma'am." The clown held out his massive hand.

"Alright, Kreepo," Crystal shook hands with the ghoulish harlequin. "Let's get scared!"

Kreepo led the trio up the metal steps and secured them in the first car of the ride. The mother of two excitedly turned to her boys to tell them not to be afraid when a massive fist crashed into her jaw and Crystal's world went black.

Crystal came to with her head hanging over the side of the ride car. She vomited. The scent of blood hung thick in the air. Shivering, the cold metal she felt beneath her told the woman she was naked. Her hands were bound to the safety rail of the ride car. The groggy mother sat up, her eyes adjusting to her black-lit surroundings. When Crystal realized the barbarity to which she awoke, her heart shattered.

"Oh, stop screaming," said Kreepo dryly. In the blacklight, the clown's face was the glowing embodiment of absurd cruelty. "You're being dramatic. We haven't even gotten to the fun part, yet!"

Colin's jaw limply shook with every word Kreepo uttered. In his outstretched right hand, he held the eleven-year-old's head by his sand-colored hair. It was no longer attached to the boy's body. Colin's eyes were gone. Streaks of caked blood stained his cheeks.

"My baby!" The words were nearly indecipherable through Crystal's screaming sobs. "What have you done to my angel?"

"I'm right here, mommy," Kreepo cooed in a sickeningly high-pitched voice as moved Colin's bottom lip to the words with his other hand. "And I'm hungry!" The clown made suckling sounds as he held Colin's head to Crystal's right nipple before callously dropping it in her lap. Crystal, shrieking like a wounded animal, harshly thrashed her body back and forth in a vain attempt at freeing herself. Kreepo slapped the frantic mother across the face with enough force her vision was filled with specks of dancing light.

"Shut up, cunt," the clown raged. "You'll ruin the fucking show!"

Crystal went silent. Her eyes stared blankly ahead in a face now devoid of emotion.

"Ladies and gentlemen, boys and girls, without further ado, let the show begin!" Kreepo started the ride. The car lurched forward, plunging Crystal into a world of horrors that grew worse with each turn of the rickety car. She saw the rotting head of a nameless hobo sat in front of a Styrofoam tombstone. The dismembered corpses of an elderly couple were strewn among rubber skeletons. Worst of all, every few feet there were gore-caked body parts Crystal recognized as belonging to Colin crudely nailed to the wall. A hand here, a leg there. Then, her baby boy's mutilated torso held by a dummy dressed as a dollar-store werewolf. When Crystal felt she couldn't take another moment, the car stopped at the final scene of the ride: the clown room.

Her sweet, six-year-old Caleb was stripped to his dinosaur briefs, splayed with his little pale arms and legs out, both hands and feet nailed to a large, black-and-white plywood hypnosis spiral. Droplets of blood gently spattered the floor. He was alive. Though his mouth was covered with duct tape, his wide, terrified eyes cried out to his mother. On either side of the spiral were mannequins dressed as twisted circus clowns.

"Please, God, don't harm my baby! *Please,*" Crystal pleaded, not breaking eye contact with her son. "I'll do anything. He's all I have left! Please!"

"Oh yes you will, but not yet." Kreepo stepped into the scene. Aside from his top hat, he was completely nude. The clown's mammoth penis was flaccid, slapping his thigh as he walked. In his left hand, he carried a butcher knife, sharp and gleaming. He reached up and yanked the tape from Caleb's mouth.

"Mommy! Mommy I'm sorry! Please don't let the clown hurt me anymore!" Caleb's small voice was shaking with terror.

Crystal screamed as Kreepo lifted the knife and in one sure stroke, sliced the boy open from his throat to his pelvis. Blood gushed to the floor as Caleb's entrails spilled from the cavity in his torso. The little boy's mouth hung agape as he looked one last time to his mother for help before the light faded from his eyes. His body convulsed once or twice more, and he was still.

The clown cupped his right hand beneath the boy's body, letting it fill with hot blood. Kreepo stroked his massive member with the ichor as it grew erect.

"Time to give daddy some pussy!" Kreepo kept stroking himself as he lurched toward a still screaming Crystal.

Catching the clown off-guard, Patrick stormed through the back door of Hell's Manor, smashing Kreepo in the side of the head with a ball peen hammer.

7

"Patrick, you cocksucker," Kreepo spat. He was lying belly up on the forest floor behind the dark ride with his wrists bound tight behind his back. His ankles were chained together. "Of course you'd ruin all my fun."

Patrick Hand stood silently over the captive clown while a man Kreepo had never seen held a flashlight aimed at him. Two other men Kreepo didn't know led a weeping Crystal from Hell's Manor to a truck. They were all dressed in a similar fashion to Patrick.

"How's Cinderella?" Kreepo grinned like an asshole, his painted face stained with blood. "That was some tight Gypsy puss—" his taunts were cut short as Patrick's boot slammed into Kreepo's ribcage, causing the clown to bolt upright.

Patrick's fist, complete with three heavy gold rings, splattered the insane clown's lips, shattering his front teeth. One of the men grabbed Kreepo's head and held it straight while another handed Patrick a roll of duct tape. Cinderella's father proceeded to wrap the tape around the clown's head several times until his mouth was entirely covered. Air escaped in ragged bursts from what little of the clown's nostrils remined exposed.

Two of the men roughly pressed the soles of their boots to Kreepo's shoulders, pinning him to the leaf-covered dirt. Patrick, staring at the clown in silence, slid his hand beneath his jacket and pulled out a black utility knife.

"As a general rule, I don't believe one man killing another," Patrick began, kneeling next to the clown and tapping his bald head with the slitted end of the box-opening tool. "It's good then, that you are more beast than man."

Kreepo's cold, black eyes stared unblinking at the wronged man.

"And I know what you want. You want me to rage, to weep, to scream at you," Patrick continued, his voice low and calm. "But I'm not here to give you what you want. What I, *we*, are here to do, is ensure a thing like you no longer walks unchecked among humanity."

Patrick gestured to the men gathering in a circle around the clown. Each held a leash attached to a stocky pit bull or rottweiler. The dogs stood perfectly still, the attention of each trained on the captive Kreepo. Placing the end of the knife above Kreepo's breastplate, Patrick used his thumb to push the slide button all the way forward, driving the blade into the clown's skin. He pressed the blade in firmly, and slowly pulled the knife down Kreepo's chest, slicing him open from just below his neck to his cock. Unmoving, Kreepo only grunted in protest. Blood poured down both sides of the clown's midsection, pooling at his sides in the dirt.

One of the men handed Patrick a knife with a longer blade. He used it to cut through Kreepo's abdominal muscle and tissue, opening a gaping hole from which his innards spilled. This made Kreepo thrash and scream against the duct tape, but the men held him tightly to the floor. The clown's eyes, once pools of cold darkness, were now desperate. Pleading. Next, Patrick used the first knife to slit open Kreepo's scrotum. When Patrick saw a testicle peeking through like a baby chick taking its first breath outside an egg, he stood and backed away.

Patrick nodded, and the men holding Kreepo in place let up and backed away, taking their places in the circle. Kreepo began writhing as if like a half-smashed cockroach, he could still make it out of his predicament alive. Patrick whistled, and the men loosed the dogs. The pack of canines was upon the clown in an instant. They went for the exposed soft bits first, hungrily chewing through intestines, testicles, and other organs with ease. For some time, the men could hear screams beneath the pile of dogs along with the sounds of snapping jaws, growling, and tearing meat. The screaming stopped when a massive rottweiler tore out the clown's throat.

When Patrick felt the dogs had their fill. He instructed the men to carefully gather the dogs. After rinsing the blood from the animals in a nearby creek, the dogs were loaded into two vans.

What remained of Kreepo was a ghastly mess. An alarming amount of the meat had been eaten from his ribcage. Most of his innards were devoured. The clown's penis and testicles were gone, as was once of his eyes, lips, and a portion of his face. Bloody neckbones were all that left between his head and body.

Patrick lifted a metal can containing gasoline and doused the clown's mangled carcass before handing it to one of his companions. He then stepped back a number of feet, lit a book of matches and tossed it onto the remains. Flames leapt, lighting the darkness as instantly, the brutalized corpse of Kreepo was set ablaze. The men stood by Patrick for a few moments before silently getting into their vehicles and disappearing into the night.

The clown burned. Muscle cooked. Fat popped and sizzled like bacon grease. Bones charred. Patrick Hand made the sign of the cross and watched the fire deep into the night.

About the Author

Jon Steffens writes boundary-pushing horror and crime fiction. He's been interested in spooky clowns since having one of the creepy bastards stare at him a little too long when he was a child at the circus with his mom and grandma. Steffens is a Splatterpunk Award-nominated author and won the 2022 Literary Nasties for "Best Collection" with The God in the Hills and Other Horrors. He lives near Fort Worth, Texas.

www.ingramcontent.com/pod-product-compliance
Ingram Content Group UK Ltd.
Pitfield, Milton Keynes, MK11 3LW, UK
UKHW020652200225
455358UK00009B/374

9 798991 961257